Sleeping Bear Press™

2395 South Huron Parkway, Suite 200
Ann Arbor, MI 48104
www.sleepingbearpress.com

Printed and bound in the United States.

10 9 8 7 6 5 4 3 2 1

Library of Congress Cataloging-in-Publication Data

Bunting, Eve, 1928-
Mr. Goat's valentine / written by Eve Bunting;
illustrated by Kevin Zimmer.
pages cm
Summary: "When Mr. Goat learns that it's Valentine's Day,
he sets out in search of gifts for his first love, but his choices
are a little unconventional"-Provided by the publisher.
ISBN 978-1-58536-944-7
[1. Valentine's Day—Fiction. 2. Gifts—Fiction. 3. Goats—Fiction.]
I. Zimmer, Kevin (Illustrator), illustrator. II. Title. III.
Title: Mister Goat's valentine.
PZ7.B91527Ms 2016
[E]—dc23
2015027634

Mr. Goat's Valentine

by Eve Bunting and Illustrated by Kevin Zimmer

Mr. Goat read the headline in the *Goat Times*.

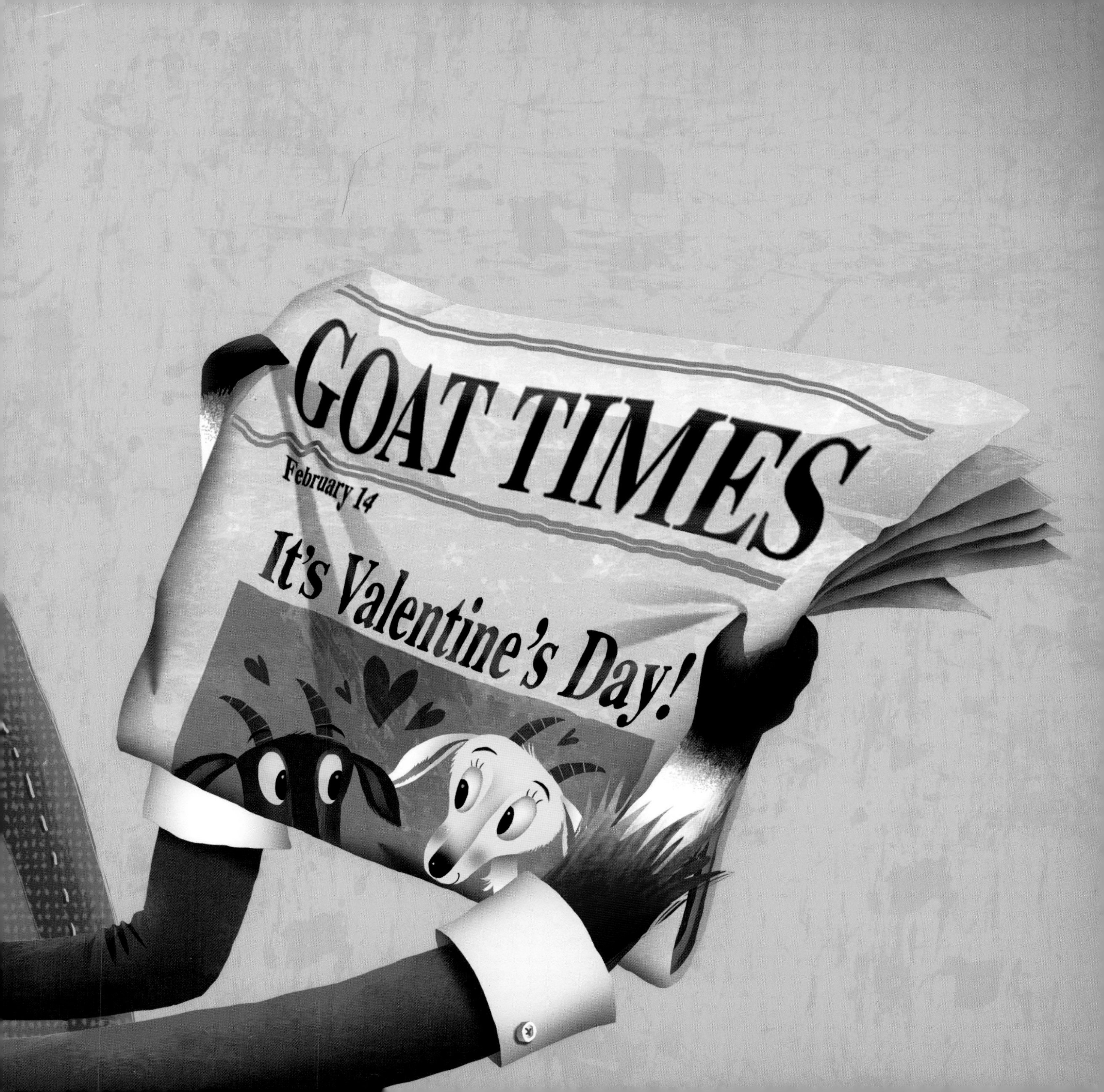
GOAT TIMES
February 14
It's Valentine's Day!

He dropped his newspaper, jumped up, got his wallet and his cell phone, and put on his bird's-nest hat.

"I'm off to show my first love how much she means to me," he told his cat, Beatrice.

"Meow," Beatrice said and yawned.

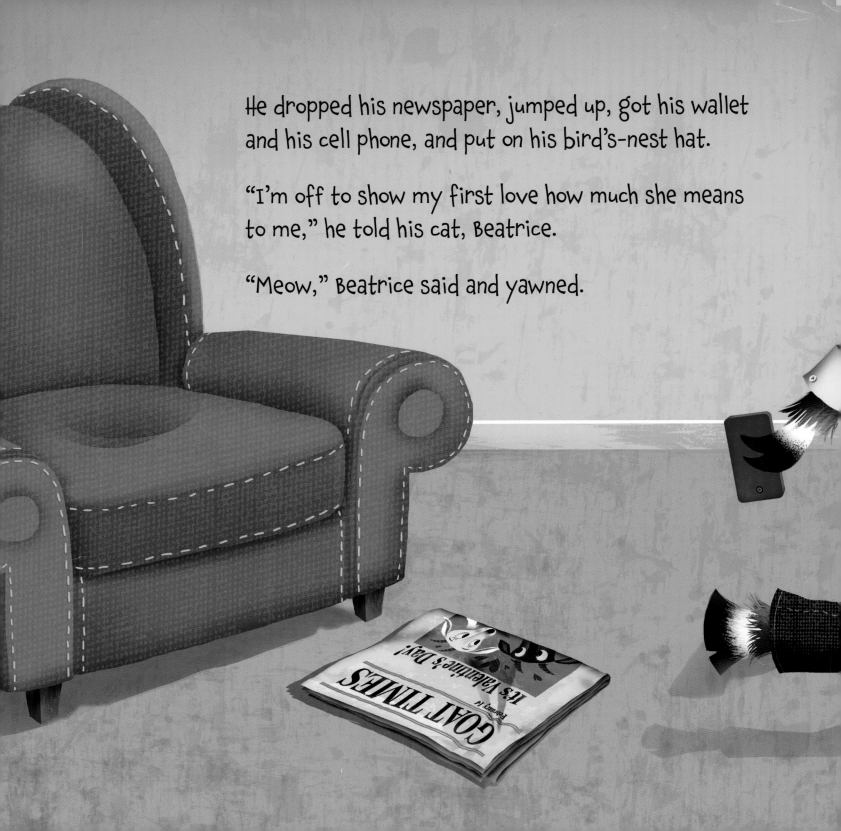

GOAT TIMES

It's Valentine's Day!

On the way Mr. Goat passed Miss Nanny Goat's weed stall.

"I'll have a mixed bouquet," Mr. Goat said. "Crabgrass, pigweeds, and ragweed in that nice, rusty can. They are for my first love. She's fond of a ragweed salad."

"She will like the can, too," Miss Nanny Goat told him.

Mr. Goat nodded. "Cans are tasty, with a sprinkle of salt."

He had only gone a few more steps when he smelled a delightful smell.

Mr. Pygmy-Little Goat had a stall under a tree. He was selling his delicious rotten eggs. He had opened one as a sample. It lay on his counter, black and oozing.

"Rotted for two years," he told Mr. Goat. "Guaranteed foul and disgusting."

Mr. Goat drooled. "I'll take four. Two for my first love and two for me. We always share."

He watched as Mr. Pygmy-Little Goat arranged them in a red box and tied the box with a pretty red ribbon.

"Perfect," Mr. Goat said. "They are so ripe I can smell them even through the shells. My first love and I will share the pretty red ribbon for dessert."

He walked on, breathing in the delightful smell of rotten eggs with every step.

Miss Skunk came by with her perfume cart. She sniffed hopefully. "What is that delicious smell?" she asked.

"Rotten eggs," Mr. Goat said.

Miss Skunk smiled. "They smell like me. May I try one?"

"Sorry." Mr. Goat wound his front legs around his egg box. "These are for my first love. It's Valentine's Day."

Miss Skunk cocked her head. "Do you have a Valentine's card for her?"

"No, I have presents."

"Too bad! For Valentine's Day you need a card."
Miss Skunk sprayed Mr. Goat.

"This is for you, Mr. Goat. You'll smell nice for her. Nice as your eggs. Happy Valentine's Day."

"Thank you, Miss Skunk."

Mr. Goat sat under a tree and thought hard.
Perhaps Miss Skunk was right.

"I do not have a card for my first love," he told himself.
"But I will compose a song and serenade her."

It was shady and cool under the tree. He sat, thinking, and before long he had the words of a song. Hurrah!

He straightened his bird's-nest hat and hurried on.

Soon he came to the house of his first love.

"Oh," he thought. "I hope she's home. I should have called first."

Mr. Goat burst into song.

When I was a little kid

It didn't matter what I did.

If I climbed too high
and fell

You'd kiss the hurt
and make it well.

You have loved me from the start

I love you with all my heart!

The door opened. And there she was.

"Happy Valentine's Day, Mother!"